This Is
CHRISTMAS

This Is CHRISTMAS

TOM BOOTH

ALADDIN JETER CHILDREN'S

New York   London   Toronto   Sydney   New Delhi

ALADDIN JETER CHILDREN'S

An imprint of Simon & Schuster Children's Publishing Division • 1230 Avenue of the Americas, New York, New York 10020 • First Aladdin hardcover edition September 2018 • Copyright © 2018 by Tom Booth • All rights reserved, including the right of reproduction in whole or in part in any form. • ALADDIN and related logo are registered trademarks of Simon & Schuster, Inc. • For information about special discounts for bulk purchases, please contact Simon & Schuster Special Sales at 1-866-506-1949 or business@simonandschuster.com. • The Simon & Schuster Speakers Bureau can bring authors to your live event. For more information or to book an event contact the Simon & Schuster Speakers Bureau at 1-866-248-3049 or visit our website at www.simonspeakers.com. • Book designed by Laura Lyn DiSiena • The illustrations for this book were rendered digitally. • The text of this book was set in Nueva Std. • Manufactured in China 0618 SCP • 2 4 6 8 10 9 7 5 3 1 • Library of Congress Control Number 2017955450 • ISBN 978-1-5344-1090-9 (hc) • ISBN 978-1-5344-1091-6 (eBook)

For my family, and Chippy

It was Christmas Eve.

Deep in the woods a little chipmunk
had a big question.

"What is Christmas, Mama?" he squeaked.

"Christmas is many things, little one.

What do you think it means?"

The little chipmunk looked around.
A badger was decorating his burrow
with bright red berries.

"Is that Christmas?" the chipmunk asked his mother.

"That's part of it," she said.

The chipmunk and his mother walked deeper
into the woods, coming to the edge of a pond.
Two ducks were sharing notes made of gold
and copper leaves.

"Is that Christmas, Mama?"

"That's part of it too," his mother said.

As they climbed a nearby tree, a family
of beetles was carrying small presents
wrapped in blades of grass.

"Is that Christmas?"

"Presents are part of Christmas,"
the chipmunk's mother told him.

From the tallest branch, the little chipmunk could see a family of geese singing carols in the sky.

"Is that Christmas, Mama?"

"Yes, that's part of it too," his mother said with a smile.

On their way back down the tree,
the little chipmunk and his mother
gathered acorns from the branches.

He thought about what he had seen
and what his mother had said.

As the moon peeked over the woods, the little chipmunk's mother tucked him into bed.

"Will I *ever* know Christmas?" he asked.
"You will in time," she whispered.

The little chipmunk closed his eyes and fell asleep, just before a chill swept past his tiny whiskers.

Outside the burrow, the wind whooshed.

The trees creaked.

The forest dreamed.

And the next morning, the little chipmunk
opened his eyes to a surprise.

He popped his head through a thick blanket of soft, sparkling snow.

The little chipmunk could no longer see the badger's berries, the ducks' notes, or the beetles' presents.

All of it was gone.

Suddenly the geese's songs rang throughout the winter sky. . . .

And all the animals gathered to sing and play together.

The little chipmunk turned to his mother.

"This is Christmas, isn't it, Mama?"

"Yes, little one.

Yes.

This is Christmas."